Animals IN DANGER

Written by Gare Thompson

STECK-VAUGHN
C O M P A N Y

A Division of Harcourt Brace & Company

www.steck-vaughn.com

Contents

Animals in Danger

There are many interesting and beautiful animals living on Earth. But some kinds are in danger. They are slowly dying out. Some die because people hunt for them. Some die because of **pollution**. Others die because they are losing the **habitat** they live in. More animals will die off if people do not keep them out of danger.

Long ago, there were many mountain gorillas. They were hunted for their skins. They were also killed and stuffed. Today there are only about six hundred of them living in the wild.

These gorillas live high up in the mountains of central Africa. The area where they live is very misty. There they eat fruits and leaves.

Mountain gorillas live in groups. The group may have one or more males, two or more females, and some young ones. Each group has a male leader. He tells the group where to go and what to do. He also **protects** them.

Gorillas travel in groups.

4

The gorilla has hair all over its body except for its face, chest, and hands.

Beluga Whales

Beluga whales must come out of the water to breathe air.

For many years, the beluga whale was a main food of the people who lived near the North Pole. Then hunters from other lands began killing many whales, too. New laws were passed to keep the whales safe, but some people have not obeyed those laws. That is why there are few beluga whales left today.

Beluga whales live in the cold Arctic Ocean waters around Canada, Alaska, and Russia. They are also called white whales because they turn white as they get older. Beluga whales grow to be about 13 feet long. They can weigh up to one ton. Many people go on whale watches to see them.

Beluga whales move their fins up and down to swim.

African Elephants

African elephants used to be hunted for their **ivory tusks**. People made jewelry, statues, and piano keys from the ivory. About ten years ago, there were only 600,000 of the elephants left. Laws were made to try to stop the hunters from killing elephants. Today workers in Africa are trying to keep the elephants safe.

The African elephant is the largest land animal. One elephant can weigh up to 16,500 pounds. An adult is about 25 feet long, including the trunk. Its trunk is a long nose that can pick up objects. Its trunk is also like a straw. The elephant draws water into its trunk and then squirts the water into its mouth.

African elephants use their trunks to drink water.

Giant Pandas

Giant pandas are one of the most popular animals in the world. But they are in danger. Hunters sell them, so there are not many left.

Giant pandas eat mostly **bamboo** shoots. Because people have moved into the land where bamboo grows, the pandas now have a hard time finding food. Pandas have less food because people are chopping down more bamboo.

Giant pandas live high in the mountains of China. These pandas are black and white. They look a bit like raccoons. They grow to be over five feet tall and weigh up to 300 pounds. There are few giant pandas left, so China has set aside some land just for them to live on.

Giant pandas live in the cool bamboo forests.

Snow Leopards

Snow leopards are beautiful cats. Their thick fur is pale gray, tan, and white. They have black or brown spots. They are hard to see in the snow.

In the past, many people hunted snow leopards for their beautiful fur. That is the main reason why they must now be protected. People have also moved into their habitat.

Snow leopards live in the coldest parts of Asia. They stay in places with snow. In the winters, they live in snowy mountain valleys. In the summers, they climb higher and higher into the tallest mountains. That way, they can live in the snow all year long.

The snow leopard's thick coat protects it from the cold in winter.

13

Hyacinth Macaws

The hyacinth macaw is a big, beautiful bird. It has very long and colorful feathers. Once these birds were hunted for their feathers to make hats. The macaws were also hunted for food.

Today there are fewer than 3,000 of these birds living. Since people will pay as much as $10,000 for a pet macaw, hunters still try to catch them. Hunters cut down trees to take the young from nests, which kills their habitat, too.

Hyacinth macaws are blue with yellow around their eyes. They are the largest parrots. They have a hooked bill for eating nuts and seeds. They live in very dry places in South America. Many macaws also live in zoos around the world.

14

The hyacinth macaw is a very colorful bird.

Bald Eagles

Most people in North America know what the bald eagle looks like. It is the national bird of the United States. It is even shown on coins and dollar bills.

Long ago, there were many bald eagles, but hunters killed most of them. Others died from polluted lakes and rivers. Today there are only about 5,000 bald eagles in the United States.

Bald eagles are part of the hawk family. They are great hunters. Eagles have good eyesight and strength. They hunt small animals and fish. Bald eagles build their nests high on rocky ledges. The high nests keep their young safe.

Bald eagles grow to be three feet long and have a **wingspan** of six feet. They have a long hooked bill and sharp claws called **talons**. The bald eagle isn't really bald. It has a white head of feathers.

The bald eagle is named for its white head.

Spotted Owls

There are only about 3,000 spotted owls living. As more trees are cut down for lumber and paper, spotted owls lose the very old trees that they build nests in. Spotted owls are also losing their habitat because of people moving into places where they live.

Spotted owls live in forests along the Pacific Ocean in Canada and the United States. They have white spots on the head and back and white bars on the chest. They sleep in the daytime and hunt mice and squirrels at night.

A spotted owl roosts in the shade to stay cool.

There are many tales about the alligator. It is a **reptile**, which is a cold-blooded animal with a backbone. In the past, hunters killed alligators for their skin. The skin was made into shoes, handbags, and other items. Then laws were passed to stop people from hunting them. Today there are more alligators, and some hunting is allowed.

The American alligator is large. It can grow up to twelve feet long. It has a long snout and many sharp teeth. It swims by moving its tail from side to side. It lives in swamps, lakes, and streams in the southern United States. Alligators eat small animals and fish. They rarely attack people.

Alligators have strong jaws. They keep their eyes above the water when they swim.

Turtles

Turtles have been on Earth since the time of the dinosaurs. Today many kinds of turtles are in danger. The turtle is the only reptile that has a shell. For years, people have hunted turtles for food and for their pretty shells.

A turtle's shell helps keep it safe. The shell is hard. Most turtles can pull their head, legs, and tail into their shell. Turtles can be as small as four inches or as large as eight feet. They have a hard beak and strong jaws for cutting food. Turtles eat plants, fish, and small animals. Most live about fifty years, but some have lived 100 years.

Turtles hatch from eggs. They lay their eggs on sandy beaches. Some people take the eggs. Pollution on the beaches also kills many eggs. Many baby turtles are taken for pets. Today some land has been set aside to keep turtles safe.

The box turtle above lives on land. The sea turtle below lives in warm waters. It comes on shore to lay eggs.

23

Komodo dragons are huge lizards with sharp claws.

Komodo Dragons

Komodo dragons are the largest lizards. They live on Komodo Island and other islands near Australia. Many died when people started taking them away from the island. People wanted them because they look a bit like dinosaurs or dragons.

People found out that Komodo dragons are dangerous. They have sharp claws and strong teeth. They can run fast. Some people have been killed by them.

Komodo dragons can grow to be ten feet long and weigh about 300 pounds. They will eat anything that moves, such as deer and pigs. The young ones protect themselves by climbing high in trees.

Today about 300 of them live on Komodo Island. It has been named a national park, so the dragons are safe there. They do not need to hunt, since they are fed in the national park.

A copper butterfly feeds on the nectar of flowers.

There are many different kinds of butterflies. Two kinds are in danger. One kind is the large copper butterfly. It is a beautiful, bright orange butterfly that lives in Europe. It is found in wet areas like marshes. Many marshes are being drained and used for farms. This means the copper butterfly has fewer places to live.

26

Karner Blue Butterflies

Another butterfly in danger is the Karner blue butterfly. This is a small butterfly. Its wings spread to about one inch. It lives in Wisconsin and several other states of the U.S.

People catch and sell them for a high price because there are so few. Also, many forests where this butterfly lives are being cut down. Butterflies feed on flowering plants in the forest. As the forests disappear, there are fewer of these butterflies left.

Karner blue butterflies look more gray than blue.

Some tarantulas live for twenty years.

Tarantulas are large, hairy spiders. They are large enough to eat frogs, lizards, and birds. Most people are afraid of them. People think that tarantulas can kill them. But in North America, no tarantula has a **venom**, or poison, that is dangerous to people. Some people like to keep these spiders as pets. Because some people capture them to sell for pets, these spiders are in danger.

This red-kneed tarantula lives in Mexico.

One of the favorite tarantulas that people want for pets is the red-kneed tarantula. This beautiful spider lives in the dry lands of Mexico. It is colorful and harmless. This makes it a good pet. People are trying to keep pet shops from selling too many tarantulas.

How to Help

Many animals are in danger, but people can help. The more people know about animals, the easier it will be to help keep them safe for the future.

People can:

• help protect animals' homes from being cut down.

• clean up polluted water and air.

• pass laws to keep hunters from hunting too many animals.

• leave animals in their natural homes and not take them as pets.

• learn more about animals and their habitats.

These organizations have more information about animals in danger.

African Wildlife Foundation
1717 Massachusetts Ave. N.W.
Suite 602
Washington, D.C. 20036
http://www.awf.org

Center for Marine Conservation
1725 DeSales Street, N.W.
Suite 500
Washington, D.C. 20036
http://riceinfo.rice.edu

National Audubon Society
700 Broadway
New York, NY 10003
http://www.igc.apc.org

World Wildlife Fund, U.S.
1250 24th Street, N.W.
Washington, D.C. 20037
http://www.wwf.org

Glossary

bamboo tall reeds

habitat the place where an animal lives

ivory tusks long, white elephant teeth

pollution dirty air or water

protects keeps from harm

reptile cold-blooded animal with a backbone, such as a snake or lizard

talons a bird's sharp claws

venom poison

wingspan the distance between the tips of a bird's or butterfly's wings when spread